WELCOME TO
PASSPORT TO READING
A beginning reader's ticket to a brand-new world!

Every book in this program is designed to build read-along and read-alone skills, level by level, through engaging and enriching stories. As the reader turns each page, he or she will become more confident with new vocabulary, sight words, and comprehension.

These PASSPORT TO READING levels will help you choose the perfect book for every reader.

READING TOGETHER
Read short words in simple sentence structures together to begin a reader's journey.

READING OUT LOUD
Encourage developing readers to sound out words in more complex stories with simple vocabulary.

READING INDEPENDENTLY
Newly independent readers gain confidence reading more complex sentences with higher word counts.

READY TO READ MORE
Readers prepare for chapter books with fewer illustrations and longer paragraphs.

This book features sight words from the educator-supported Dolch Sight Words List. This encourages the reader to recognize commonly used vocabulary words, increasing reading speed and fluency.

For more information, please visit passporttoreadingbooks.com.

Enjoy the journey!

marvelkids.com

© 2018 MARVEL

Illustrations by Steve Kurth

Cover design by Elaine Lopez-Levine. Cover illustration by Steve Kurth.

Little, Brown and Company
Hachette Book Group
1290 Avenue of the Americas, New York, NY 10104
Visit us at LBYR.com
marvelkids.com

First Edition: January 2018

Little, Brown and Company is a division of Hachette Book Group, Inc.
The Little, Brown name and logo are trademarks of Hachette Book Group, Inc.

The publisher is not responsible for websites (or their content)
that are not owned by the publisher.

Library of Congress Control Number 2017954821

ISBNs: 978-0-316-41315-2 (pbk.), 978-0-316-41312-1 (ebook),
978-0-316-41314-5 (ebook), 978-0-316-41317-6 (ebook)

Printed in the United States of America

CW

10 9 8 7 6 5

Passport to Reading titles are leveled by independent reviewers applying the standards developed by Irene Fountas and Gay Su Pinnell in *Matching Books to Readers: Using Leveled Books in Guided Reading*, Heinemann, 1999.

MARVEL

BLACK PANTHER

MEET BLACK PANTHER

ADAPTED BY R. R. BUSSE

ILLUSTRATIONS STEVE KURTH

PRODUCED BY KEVIN FEIGE, P.G.A.

DIRECTED BY RYAN COOGLER

WRITTEN BY RYAN COOGLER &
JOE ROBERT COLE

LITTLE, BROWN AND COMPANY
New York   Boston

Attention, Black Panther fans!
Look for these words when you read
this book. Can you spot them all?

beads

fighter

doctor

chase

This is Black Panther!

He is also named T'Challa.

He is the next king of Wakanda.

He has a special suit and

is very smart.

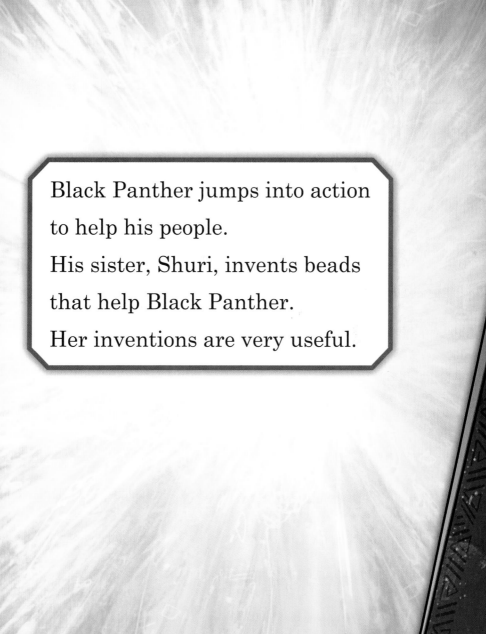

Black Panther jumps into action to help his people.

His sister, Shuri, invents beads that help Black Panther.

Her inventions are very useful.

T'Challa stops the bad guys!

His plans always work.

He is very fast.

Then he sees Nakia.

They were friends when they were kids.

She is on a mission for Wakanda, too.

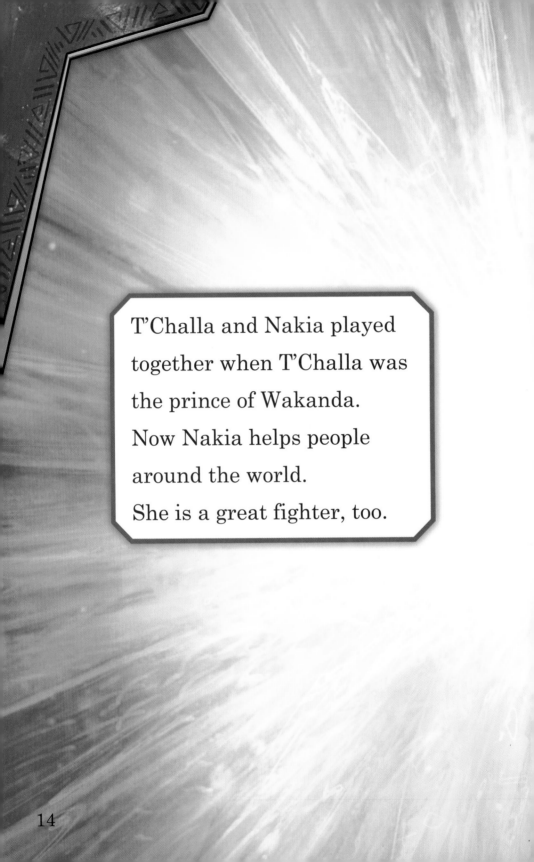

T'Challa and Nakia played
together when T'Challa was
the prince of Wakanda.
Now Nakia helps people
around the world.
She is a great fighter, too.

T'Challa is happy to go back home.

He talks to his mother, Ramonda.

They remember his father.

T'Chaka was a great king.

He and Ramonda raised T'Challa to do what is right.

While he is home in Wakanda, T'Challa talks to his sister, Shuri. Shuri is so smart!
She makes all of Black Panther's gadgets.

She makes T'Challa a brand-new Black Panther suit.
This suit absorbs attacks!

Now T'Challa must become the king of Wakanda. He must fight without his suit! He must fight without his super strength!

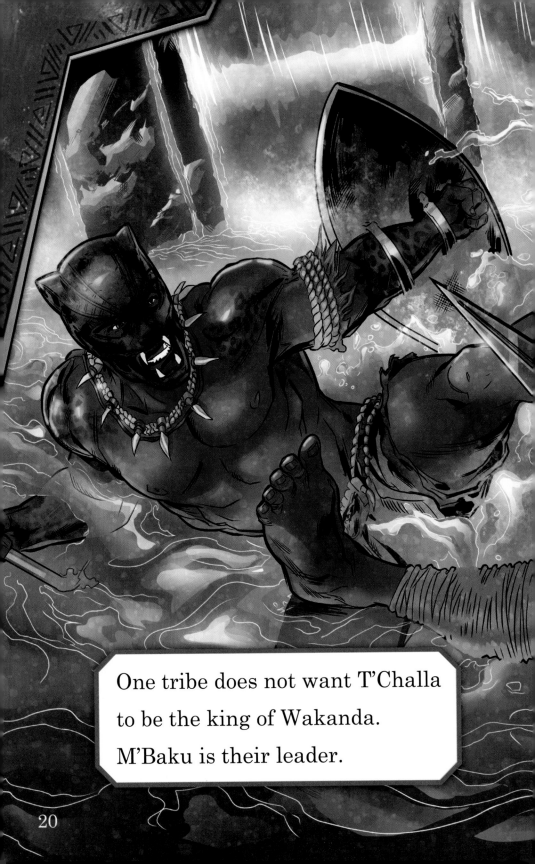

One tribe does not want T'Challa to be the king of Wakanda. M'Baku is their leader.

He fights T'Challa to see
who will be the king.
Everyone watches.

After his fight, T'Challa needs to rest.
Zuri takes care of him.
He is the best doctor in the Golden City.
He restores T'Challa's strength and
talks about his father.

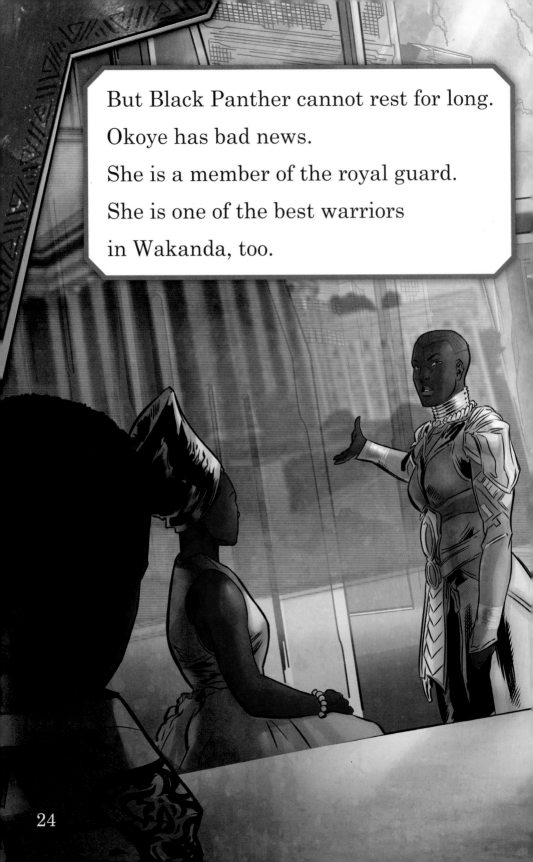

But Black Panther cannot rest for long.
Okoye has bad news.
She is a member of the royal guard.
She is one of the best warriors
in Wakanda, too.

Ulysses Klaue stole something important!
It is Wakandan vibranium!
T'Challa must catch Klaue.

Erik Killmonger will do anything to help Klaue.

He wants money and power.

He helps Klaue try to sell the vibranium.

CIA agent Everett Ross sets a trap!

He catches the villains.

Ross is friends with T'Challa.

Klaue and Killmonger try to escape the trap.

Luckily, Black Panther is close!

Black Panther will not let them get away.

The chase is on!
Can Black Panther catch
Klaue and save Wakanda?

MARVEL
BLACK PANTHER

LOOK FOR THESE OTHER BLACK PANTHER BOOKS!

THE JUNIOR NOVEL
&
ON THE PROWL!

Black Panther is going to be
the next king of Wakanda.
Visit his country, and
meet his family and foes!

CHECKPOINTS IN THIS BOOK ✔

WORD COUNT	GUIDED READING LEVEL	NUMBER OF DOLCH SIGHT WORDS
403	K	70

READING TOGETHER 1

READING OUT LOUD 2

READING INDEPENDENTLY 3

READY TO READ MORE 4

Look inside for more about
Passport to Reading!
Visit passporttoreadingbooks.com

VISIT US AT
LBYR.com

$4.99 U.S. / $6.49 CAN.
ISBN 978-0-316-41315-2

9 780316 413152

5 0 4 9 9 >